THE HAPPY PRINCE

THE HAPPY PRINCE

From the Fairy Tale by Oscar Wilde

JANE RAY

🌳 ORCHARD BOOKS 🌳

For Joseph, my own little Happy Prince.

J.R.

Orchard Books
96 Leonard Street, London EC2A 4RH
Orchard Books Australia
14 Mars Road, Lane Cove, NSW 2066
ISBN 1 85213 619 7 (hardback)
ISBN 1 86039 092 7 (paperback)
First published in Great Britain 1994
First paperback publication 1996
Illustrations © Jane Ray 1994
The right of Jane Ray to be identified as the Illustrator
of the Work has been asserted by her in accordance
with the Copyright, Design and Patents Act, 1988.
A CIP catalogue record for this book is available
from the British Library.
Printed in Belgium

High above the city, on a tall column, stood the statue of the Happy Prince. He was gilded all over with thin leaves of fine gold, for eyes he had two bright sapphires, and a large red ruby glowed on his sword-hilt.

One night there flew over the city a little Swallow. He saw
the statue on the tall column. So he alighted just between
the feet of the Happy Prince.

"I have a golden bedroom," he said to himself, and he prepared
to go to sleep; but just as he was putting his head under his wing,
a large drop of water fell on him. Then another drop fell.
A third drop fell, and he looked up.

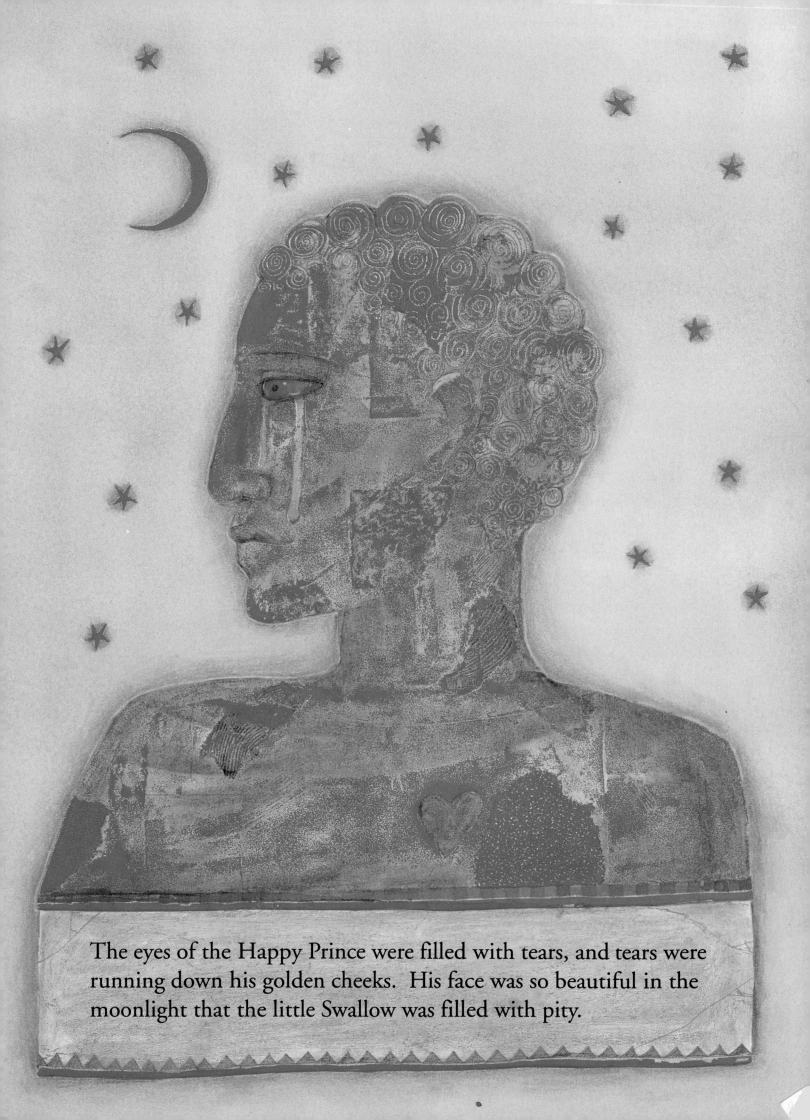

The eyes of the Happy Prince were filled with tears, and tears were running down his golden cheeks. His face was so beautiful in the moonlight that the little Swallow was filled with pity.

"Who are you?" he said.

"I am the Happy Prince."

"Why are you weeping then?" asked the Swallow. "You have quite drenched me."

"When I was alive and had a human heart," answered the statue, "I did not know what tears were. My courtiers called me the Happy Prince. And now that I am dead, they have set me here so high that I can see all the misery of my city, and though my heart is made of lead I cannot choose but weep."

"Far away," continued the statue, "is a poor house. In a bed a little boy is lying ill. He is asking for oranges. His mother has nothing to give him but river water, so he is crying. Swallow, little Swallow, will you not bring her the ruby out of my sword-hilt?"

"I am waited for in Egypt," said the Swallow. "My friends are flying up and down the Nile, and talking to the lotus flowers. Soon they will go to sleep in the tomb of the great King. The King is there himself in his painted coffin. Round his neck is a chain of pale green jade, and his

hands are like withered leaves."

"Swallow, Swallow, little Swallow," said the Prince, "will you not stay with me for one night, and be my messenger?"

The Happy Prince looked so sad that the little Swallow picked out the great ruby from the Prince's sword, and flew away with it in his beak over the roofs of the town.

He passed by the cathedral tower, where the white marble angels were sculptured. He passed over the river, and saw the lanterns hanging to

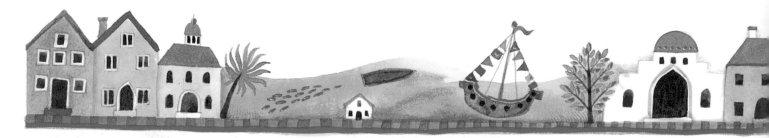

the masts of the ships. At last he came to the poor house where the little boy lay ill and dropped the ruby onto the table.

Then he flew back to the Happy Prince, and told him what he had done. "It is curious, but I feel quite warm now, although it is so cold."

When the moon rose the next day the Swallow looked up at the Happy Prince. "I am just starting for Egypt," he said.

"Swallow, Swallow, little Swallow," said the Prince, "will you not stay with me one night longer?"

"I am waited for in Egypt," answered the Swallow. "There, on a great granite throne sits the god Memnon. All night long he watches the stars, and when the morning star shines he utters one cry of joy, and then is silent. At noon the yellow lions come down to the water's edge to drink."

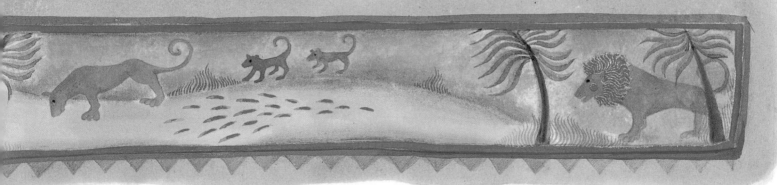

"Swallow, Swallow, little Swallow," said the Prince, "far away across the city I see a young man in a garret. He is trying to finish a play for the Director of the Theatre, but he is too cold to write any more."

"I will wait with you one night longer," said the Swallow, who really had a good heart. "Shall I take him another ruby?"

"Alas! I have no ruby now," said the Prince. "My eyes are all that I have left. They are made of rare sapphires from India. Pluck one of them out and take it to him."

"Dear Prince," said the Swallow, "I cannot do that," and he began to weep.

"Swallow, Swallow, little Swallow," said the Prince, "do as I command you."

So the Swallow plucked out the Prince's eye, and flew away to the student's garret. And when the student looked up he found the sapphire lying on his desk.

"I must bid you goodbye," cried the Swallow, when the moon rose the next night. "I am going to Egypt!"

"Swallow, Swallow, little Swallow," said the Prince, "will you not stay with me one night longer?"

"It is winter," answered the Swallow, "and the snow will soon be here. In Egypt the sun is warm on the palm trees and the crocodiles lie in the mud and look lazily about them. Dear Prince, I must leave you, but next spring I will bring you back two beautiful jewels in place of those you have given away."

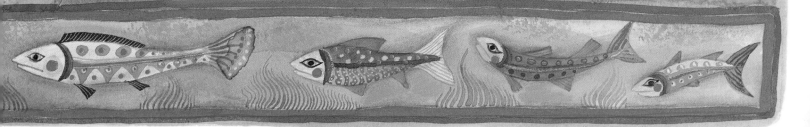

"In the square below," said the Happy Prince, "there stands a little match girl. She has let her matches fall in the gutter. She has no shoes or stockings, and her little head is bare. Pluck out my other eye, and give it to her."

"I will stay with you one night longer," said the Swallow, "but I cannot pluck out your eye. You would be quite blind then."

"Swallow, Swallow, little Swallow," said the Prince, "do as I command you."

So the Swallow plucked out the Prince's other eye, darted down with it and slipped the jewel right into the palm of the little match girl's hand.

Then the Swallow came back to the Prince. "You are quite blind now," he said, "so I will stay with you always."

All the next day he sat on the Prince's shoulder, and told him stories of what he had seen in strange lands. He told him of the red ibises, who stand in long rows on the banks of the Nile, and catch goldfish in their beaks;

of the Sphinx, who is as old as the world itself, and lives in the desert, and knows everything;

of the great green snake that sleeps in a palm tree;

and of the King of the Mountains of the Moon, who is as black as ebony, and worships a large crystal.

"Dear little Swallow," said the Prince, "you tell me of marvellous things, but there is no mystery so great as misery. Fly over my city, little Swallow, and tell me what you see there."

So the Swallow flew over the great city and saw the rich merry-making
in their beautiful houses while the beggars were sitting at the gates.
Then he flew back and told the Prince what he had seen.

"I am covered with fine gold," said the Prince. "You must take it off, leaf by leaf, and give it to the poor."

Leaf after leaf of the fine gold the Swallow picked off, till the Happy Prince looked quite dull and grey. Leaf after leaf of the fine gold he brought to the poor, and the children's faces grew rosier, and they laughed and played games in the street.

Then the snow came, and after the snow came the frost. Everybody went about in furs, and the little boys wore scarlet caps and skated on the ice.

The poor little Swallow grew colder and colder, but he would not leave the Prince. He loved him too well.

But at last he knew he was going to die. "Goodbye, dear Prince!" he murmured. And he kissed the Happy Prince and fell down dead at his feet.

At that moment a curious crack sounded inside the statue. The leaden heart had snapped right in two. It certainly was a dreadfully hard frost.

Early next morning the Mayor was walking in the square below with his town councillors. "Dear me! How shabby the Happy Prince looks!" he said. "And there is actually a dead bird at his feet!" he continued. "We must issue a proclamation that birds are not allowed to die here."

So they pulled down the statue of the Happy Prince. Then they melted the statue in a furnace. But the broken heart would not melt, so it was thrown on a dust heap, where the dead Swallow was also lying.

"Bring me the two most precious things in the city," said God to one of his angels; and the angel brought him the leaden heart and the dead bird.

"You have rightly chosen," said God, "for in my garden of Paradise this little bird shall sing and the Happy Prince shall live for ever more."

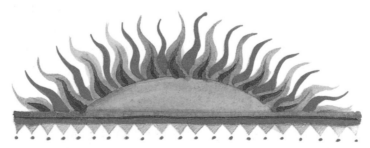